LIFE IN THE TWENTIES:

The Good, Bad & Ugly

TIEANNA DENAE

Printed in the United States of America
First Printing: July 2022
The Scribe Tribe Publishing Group

ISBN-978-1-958436-02-8 (print)
ISBN – 978-1-958436-03-5 (ebook)

This book is dedicated to my beautiful cousin/friend/
sister all in one, Tanisha Freeman. I hope I've made
you proud with my accomplishments. I love you and
miss you. Keep watching over us.

Contents

Picture Perfect 1

Death Comes Knocking 5

Get Back Up and Try Again 11

      The Big Day 13

Fading Away 17

Fighting Pride 25

      Home Sweet Home 27

Second Time's The Charm 31

Girls Night Out 35

He loves me. He loves me not. 39

When Life Throws You Lemons.... 47

Jayceon Douglass. 49

Time Will Tell 53

Decisions, Decisions. 55

    First Response 56

    New Chapter. 58

    The Question. 59

Chapter 29 63

Meet the Author. 67

PICTURE PERFECT

Hi, my name is Harper Johnson, but everyone calls me Harp, Kittie (a nickname given to me by my late great-grandma) or H.P. I was born and raised in Columbus, Georgia but I currently reside in Dallas, Texas. I'm 29 years old. Yes! Twenty-nine! But it feels like I'm twice my age. I'm not sure if that's the maturity in me or if that's because I've been through so much already. From failing school, changing careers, losing loved ones, battling depression, self-esteem issues and let's not forget failed relationships. Have you ever felt like you were too old to not have it all together but at the same time you were too young to have it all together? That's how I've felt. Trying to plan your life out but it doesn't always go as planned? Yes, I've been there too.

When I was in elementary school, my teachers would give me old tests, old lesson plans and any extra papers that weren't being used and I would collect them and play "teachers" with it. I always thought I would be a teacher, specifically a 5th grade math teacher because I was so good at math. Funny how things change. My sophomore year of high school I became a certified nurse assistant so my passion for nursing took off from there. You see, life doesn't always go as planned. People say enjoy your twenties, but in my opinion, your twenties can be a stressful time period because you are still trying to find your way in this thing called life.

After I graduated high school in 2011, I attended Columbus Technical College. I knew that I wanted to continue my nursing career, so I started taking the prerequisite courses that were necessary for the practical nursing program. A year after that, I received my acceptance letter and started the program. Nursing school wasn't easy. It was intense. I had to remain focused 24/7. There was no time to lack. I felt like I no longer had a life, a social life. I was 20 years old, wishing I was picking out my outfit for the party that Friday night. Instead, I was studying the steps on how to insert a nasogastric tube because I had a practicum the following Monday. I felt like I should have been living life and enjoying my 20's, but I was enrolled in that program, so I had to remain focused. And although all I did was focus throughout my high school years, it was what I had to continue to do. I never quite experienced the "fun life." But I had to push through.

Each week that went by was filled with anxiety. The closer it got to graduation, the more challenging it became. Nursing school was no joke but I had pushed through and made it to finals. Something about the words "finals" intimidated me and made my stomach turn. I impatiently waited for my final grade to be posted onto Blackboard. It seemed like the longest 10 minutes of my life. To my surprise, I had failed my maternity and pediatrics exam. I was shocked. I didn't feel the need to worry much about the maternity final because I was confident, so I thought. I had spent more time drilling the signs and symptoms of a patient who is experiencing hypoglycemia than worrying about at what age the anterior fontanelle closes on an infant. We had to have an 80% in all classes in order to graduate. I had a 79.4! Talk about devastation. It would be a year before I could go back to retake the course. I felt like a failure. I couldn't believe I had failed. I was disappointed in myself. Most of all, I was embarrassed. What would people say? My family? People at my job? I felt like I had let my family down along with myself. I didn't know where I would go from there.

I didn't plan on failing. Failing was not in my agenda. I had planned everything out, but I guess that's the big lesson in all of this. It's not my plan. It's God's plan. After a few weeks of me beating myself up and realizing I had come so far, I knew I couldn't give up. So, I decided to go back to school the next year.

DEATH COMES KNOCKING

Making the decision to return to school the following January of 2014 to finish the program seemed like the smartest thing to do. After all, I had come so far, and I didn't want to just throw it away. Meanwhile, in September of 2013 I had moved into my first apartment with my *at-the-time boyfriend*, Darius Jones aka "Big D." Darius and I had been together since we were 15 and 17 years old. He was two years older than me. I guess you can say we were high school sweethearts. Darius was very well known. I mean everyone knew him. In school, I was more to myself so when we started dating, I guess you can say I became somewhat "known" too. He had gone off to college after he graduated but now he was back home; school wasn't really his thing. Having him back home, both of us were in a better place and we were ready to branch out on our own. I mean being in our own place and working; I felt like I was living the life. Not to mention, my closest friends stayed in the same apartment complex. We would refer to ourselves as the *Real Housewives of Brook Landon* because we all had been in long lasting relationships. There were my best friends, Desiree and Tevin; they stayed in the next building. To the right of them was Victoria and Deandre and in the next section was Brianna and Xzavier. Xzavier was Darius' best friend and eventually Brianna and I became close as well. We were at each other's houses every weekend. Cooking, partying, just having a blast. It was the same thing over and over, work and figuring out which couple would host the next gathering. Time surely went fast before I knew it, it was November. I was excited because as each month went by that meant that it was getting closer to finishing the program.

One evening, I had this horrible feeling that something was going to happen the next day. I had a doctor's appointment the following morning, but I had a feeling I wouldn't make it. That next morning, I received the worst call of my life. My homegirl Binky called me at 6:15am. I was asleep so I decided that I would call her back later that day. I was thinking maybe she was asking who was driving to work because we would car pull but then I thought it was too early for her to call about work being that we didn't work until three that afternoon. I tried to fall asleep but something kept telling me I needed to see what she was calling about. So I returned her phone call.

"What's up Bink, you called?" I could hear what sounded like crying and police sirens.

"It's Andrea..something has happened, HP."

I dropped the phone. My heart sunk down to my feet. Bink had informed me that something terrible had taken place at our homegirl Andrea's house. Binky stayed in the same apartment complex as Drea. I knew it was bad. At that point I was discombobulated. I don't think I even said two words to D because I was running out of my front door. I called Desiree and caught her up on the news and before I could hang up the phone she was running out her door heading to my car. We did 90 in a 55 all the way to their apartment complex. They lived about 15 minutes from us in Forest Woods Apartments, but before we arrived at the apartment complex Bink was calling back to tell us that they had pronounced Drea deceased. I felt stuck. I couldn't put this into reality.

This can't be real, I thought. *This cannot be happening. I see this on television, but this cannot be happening in real life. Not my friend. Not my friend.* But it was true.

When we arrived at the apartment complex there were people everywhere. Some were crying and screaming. Some were making phone calls. Some were looking like me.... as if they were trying to figure out if this was real or a nightmare. Reality hit as I watched the coroner bring out Drea's lifeless body. She had been murdered by her abusive boyfriend in such a vicious way. This not only affected those close to her, but it shook the entire city. Andrea was one of those people that really left a positive mark on every person she encountered. After her funeral, depression kicked in like a ton of bricks. I felt like I wasn't alive. I was just existing. I was angry. I was hurt and confused. I couldn't understand how someone could do that. I knew I was falling into deep depression. It just felt like a dark cloud was looming above my head and no sunshine could penetrate through to my world. I knew I needed help and fast! I decided that I needed to talk to a therapist–someone I didn't know, not my friends, not my family, not even D but someone I could express how I felt without judgment. I had fallen so deeply that I no longer felt like I had a purpose. I was truly broken. Not only was I depressed but I had developed some form of anxiety. To even do the dishes was an issue for me. When I would come across a knife, I would shake and feel nervous. I remember one day as I was driving to work, I saw yellow crime scene tape surrounding the perimeter of a house and I felt like my stomach was going to fall to my feet. Tachycardia kicked in because I could feel my heart pounding and beating away. The therapist taught me different ways to cope and how to deal with my anxiety. And although it helped some, it didn't take the pain away. The prescribed medicine just induced sleep. I was still in trouble, and I knew I couldn't go on any longer.

One night I sat in the bathtub, Mary Mary playing in the background, and I laid back and talked to God as if He was right in front of me. That is when I had my own personal experience, and I knew that God was indeed real. You know, growing up I went to church, and I believed in God, but at that moment I had my first personal proof that He was who He was. I asked Him to deliver me from depression. I asked Him to give me peace. I asked Him to let me wake up the next morning and feel like I had a purpose. A purpose to live and a purpose to fight depression. When I opened my eyes the next morning, the sun was shining brightly. I felt a sense of peace. I opened my blinds. An overwhelming feeling of strength and preparedness came over me; I was ready to tackle the world and get my life back. And so, I did.

GET BACK UP AND TRY AGAIN

In January of 2014, I started school again. I was working full time and going to class. With a home to care for, I was still responsible for bills. Class was every Monday and clinicals were on Tuesdays and Thursdays. Clinicals gave us that hands-on experience at different nursing home facilities and hospitals. Being a student and working full time was a challenge but with Darius' support, he made it a bit easier. Clinicals were from 6:30am-2:30pm. I lived about four minutes from the hospital and the nursing home facility that we attended, and I would get home, change into my work uniform and head straight to work from 3:30-11pm. Study time was on my days off and when I was able to have a little "down-time" at work. Classes ended at the end of April, and I passed my maternity and pediatric exam! Now that finals were over, it was time for the pinning ceremony.

The pinning ceremony was a ceremony that welcomed us into the nursing profession. We received a pin and a lamp.

The lamp was included as a representation of the late Florence Nightingale. A few days later was the actual graduation. "Harper Denae Johnson," the voice of the dean of nursing calling my name was music to my ears. As I walked across the stage to receive my certificate, I could hear my family yelling, especially my mom because she was naturally loud.

"Go Kittie, that's momma baby!"

Desiree and another friend of ours were also in the nursing program so it was even more exciting. It was everything I could have imagined except one thing. My dad. My dad always popped in and out of my life. But I was really hoping that he would follow through with his promises this time. I had given him an invitation to my graduation, and he was a no show. No text, no call, no nothing. But I wasn't going to let that ruin my moment. I was overjoyed. I finally accomplished something. I finally made my family proud.

Now it was time to prepare for the National Council Licensure Examination (NCLEX). This test is a nationwide examination for the licensing of nurses in the US. This exam determined if I was going to be a nurse or not. Yes, I had the certificate, but the work was not over. The NCLEX was not like a regular 50 question exam. It was a timed 80-question to 205-question test. This test isn't just about knowing about a medical condition or knowing how to administer a medication, but the test is also created to test your critical thinking and how to apply your knowledge to nursing situations. This test is serious because when you are licensed, you are now in charge of someone else's life. I felt like I needed more time to prepare. So, I waited a few months after I graduated to take it. After graduating, the board of nursing allows upcoming NCLEX examiners to work as an LPN in training for 90 days so I switched positions at my job.

The Big Day

The day was August 17, 2014. I arrived at the testing site and I felt the intensity and the severity of the test before I even began to take it. Checking in was a 15-minute process. We had to show two forms of identification and take a photo to store in their system. I had to put my purse in a locker and empty out my pockets. They even looked at my glasses. I asked the lady why she had done so and she told me I would be surprised at some of the hiding places that they had come across after finding cheat sheets from previous testers. After thoroughly searching me, she escorted me to the testing room. The proctor went through the rules and regulations, and she said the words that I'm not so sure if I was ready to hear at that time.

"Good luck. You may begin."

Luck was what I needed but I'm not so sure if I was actually ready to begin. I was a nervous wreck. My palms were sweating. All I could hear was the clock reminding me that time was moving forward even if I was stuck.

Tic tok, tic tok, tic tok.

The test timer continued as I forged through question after question. At question number 80, my computer just shut off. I had only been in that small room for one hour and thirty minutes. *There's no way I could be finished! Did I pass? Did I fail? Lord, please let me pass!* A world of thoughts danced through my head that day and then on into the evening. I spent all night researching how to know if I passed or failed. Two days later, I logged into the website, biting my nails, sitting on the edge of the chair, legs shaking while the website loaded. The page and finally it popped up. **FAILED.**

There is no way this can be. God, how can this be? I failed the class. You let me get back into the program to retake the class and I graduated just to let me fail the NCLEX?

I was so angry. Angry at myself and at God too. I felt humiliated. I was yet again disappointing my family and giving people at my job something to talk about. You know how people talk. And always have something to say when you do bad but would hardly open their mouth when you do good.

Yup, that was the people at my job... well some of them anyway. I felt like I had completely wasted my time. At only 21 years old, I thought about how I could have been at a university living the college life, going to the clubs and turning up. *And yet, here I am, at home, failing my board exam. What a waste of time!* I decided at that point I wasn't wasting my time any longer.

FADING AWAY

Things got rocky in my relationship. Going on year seven, things just started going south. Darius and I were no longer seeing eye to eye. I felt like he didn't understand me, and he felt like I didn't understand him, although neither one of us made it easy to talk to one another. I'll be honest. I did start to fall dependent on him. I wasn't completely pulling my weight of the bills, and I also started hanging out with the girls more than usual. I wanted to be on the scene of every party. Didn't want to miss a beat. But at that moment I felt like I deserved a break, and he should understand. After all, he was able to experience college life. Besides, I had been there for him as well. Maybe not as much financially because he made the most money. However, it was me that got us the apartment, and it was my car that we shared for years before he was able to get his own. Speaking of when he got his own car, that toyota was always in the wind. Every chance he got. Didn't see much of him.

As time went on, we continued to drift apart. Amongst other issues, I wasn't the same person anymore and neither was he.

We both had a difficult time adjusting to who we had grown to be. It was hard for us to communicate without it turning into a big fight. We just didn't click anymore. We tried to work on things but we both felt like neither of us was listening to each other. Darius was no saint. He had ways about him that weren't so easy to deal with. He felt like I should accept it because that's just the way he was. But I disagreed. I needed to see a change but as weeks went on, things in our home got worse. Home didn't feel like home. Neither one of us were happy. There were days when I had to give myself a pep talk on the way to work, drilling in my mind not to make it noticeable that I had been crying and not to make it obvious that something was bothering me. There were nights where I was left sleeping alone. I would text or call but there was no answer. And the fact that we were no longer being intimate on the regular was a big red flag for me. I mean I would walk around the house in my sexy panties, and he wouldn't even budge. I would leave the house without giving him a kiss and he did nothing. Prior to that, Darius would make sure I wouldn't leave as far as going to the mailbox without me giving him a kiss, so when he seemed to not care at all, I knew it was something up. It was just a matter of time before I would find out.

Time and time again, I prayed for God to fix us. We had been together for seven years and that was quite an investment of time to just throw it away. But it seemed like the more I prayed the worse it got. One day after work, Victoria and I were going to Brianna's house for a 'kickback' as we called it. I had gotten home from work, showered and was getting dressed. As I headed out the door, I stumbled across a necklace. I examined the necklace, and it was clear that it was a female's because it was the shape of a heart with pink stones, but that female was NOT Harper Johnson. I placed the necklace on the nightstand and kept going. Reality didn't hit me until later that night as I reminisced over the scenario that had taken place an hour ago. The necklace. The fact that it belonged to another female and the biggest question of them all—where the hell was Darius and why hadn't he returned my phone call? Even Xzavier was looking for him. At first, I thought he must know where D is, but it was clear to me that he was just as clueless as I was.

I tried hard to pull myself together. I didn't want anyone to notice that I was seconds away from spazzing out and crying a river. I stepped outside Bri and Xzavier's apartment to wipe my face and gain my composure. I felt the breeze of the air coming from inside the apartment so I knew someone had stepped out. It was Bri and Victoria asking me if I was okay. I told them yes, but I knew they could tell that was a lie because I then burst out in tears. Patting me on my back and giving me encouraging words, they were able to calm me down and we headed back inside. You ever felt like your body was somewhere, but your mind was not? That's how I felt. That whole night. I was in my friend's apartment, but my mind was in all sorts of places.

When Darius got home the next morning, he asked me if I had seen a necklace because his homegirl had come over. Now this was a homegirl I had never met before. Don't get me wrong, I was cool with D having friends of the opposite sex but I knew them all. So, when he told me about this random chick, I didn't believe him for one second. He told me that ole girl had come over to purchase his latest mixtape. Darius was an inspiring rapper who was known in our city. He had been into music ever since he was in diapers. That's another thing that drew me into him, his passion for music. I loved to listen to him. Not only could he rap but he could out-sang John Legend anyday. I would try to sing along with him. I couldn't hold a note but, in my mind, you couldn't tell me that I wasn't the next Jasmine Sullivan. So, when he told me about his "homegirl" coming over to purchase his mixtape that sounded logical. But what was her necklace doing on our bedroom floor, and furthermore, how did it come off her neck? She told D that the necklace was broken so it was nothing new for it to come off. He kept his mixtapes in our walk-in closet that was also in our bedroom so that justified why it was found on the bedroom floor. I let it go but in my mind, I was taking notes.

He told me his homegirl didn't stay near us so he would just give it to his homeboy to give to her because they were closer in distance. Days went by and I was on top of everything. Darius, or should I say "sneaky D," had placed the necklace in our spare bedroom in a little T-Mobile box that his old phone had come in. Every time he would say he was going out, I would check the box to see if the necklace was gone because that would let me know he was going to meet up with ole girl. I knew he was lying about his homeboy meeting her and returning the jewelry. That just didn't make sense. One evening he told me that he had to take his mom to her doctor's appointment. I went to check the box and it was empty. I knew that he was going to meet up with her. I felt it in my spirit that he was lying about his mother's appointment, but I wasn't ready. I wasn't ready to face the fact that D could betray me.

Sure, we had our issues. Sure, I had fallen off and went through a phase but to step outside our relationship, no one could pay me to do that. I just knew that I had meant much more to him than that. So, I kept trying to see if things would get better and things just kept getting worse with us. I couldn't do it any longer. I told God I was ready to accept whatever it was. That same day I prayed for answers, I found out that he had indeed stepped outside our relationship. I had driven his car to go to the grocery store when I noticed a pair of cheap looking, laced underwear in between the passenger seat and the center console and they weren't mine. I could see the tag sticking out as they were inside out and they were a size medium. I was a fluffy girl. There was no way that I could even get a thigh in those things. It was almost as if he wanted me to find them...or perhaps she did. I whipped his car around so fast you would have thought I was in the *Fast and Furious* movie with Paul Walker.

I pulled up in front of our apartment and took a deep breath to prepare myself for the hurt. I knew deep down inside D was cheating but it still hurt when those thoughts became more a reality. I went into our bedroom where D was asleep. A part of me wanted to get a pot of cold water and throw it on him to wake him up, but I decided to stay as contactless as possible. He had awakened because slammed the keys on the dresser.

Yoooo, Harp what are you doing, what's your problem?

I'm going to give you 5 seconds to tell me the truth, D. Are you cheating on me?

There was complete silence. Darius was NEVER lost for words so for him to be quiet spoke volumes. Since a cat seemed to have caught his tongue, I then presented him with the underwear I had found to see if they could bring him out of this amnesia state he seemed to have developed so suddenly. He took a deep breath and told me to sit down, I declined and told him I would rather stand. He inhaled and exhaled once again and to my surprise words started flowing out his mouth. He proceeded to tell me that we had fallen off and our relationship had taken a toll on him. As tears flowed down his cheeks, he said that he felt like we had drifted apart and that he didn't want to just up and leave. He told me that ole girl had become someone he confided in about us and that his feelings for her had deepened. He admitted to being intimate with her. D kept talking but all that seemed to repeat in my head was the fact that he had sex with that girl.

"Harp..Harp are you okay? Say something please!"

"How could you do this, D?"

I was extremely hurt. I was more hurt that he didn't come to me prior to making the decision to sleep with her and disrespecting our relationship. I've always made it clear that if either of us ever felt like we needed to take a break or that we wanted to end things, we would come to one another before betraying the other person. So, for him to not do that hurt me more. I was feeling how he felt as far as us heading in two different directions, but our relationship meant so much more. I was a girl true to my words. I've always told him if he cheated, I would be done. So, I knew then that it was over for us and it was. We knew deep down inside that it had been over for a while, but we were just hanging on.

FIGHTING PRIDE

Because we were living together and he didn't want to leave me with the bills, we agreed to give each other a few months to get ourselves together to prepare financially to separate. Things were awkward at times, but we had grown to accept our situation. We had become somewhat best friends. People would ask me how I could be so cool with someone that had hurt me. Two words. GROWTH and FORGIVENESS. It took time. It didn't happen overnight. Trust me, there were times when I couldn't stand the sight of D, but it took understanding and honesty. We knew our time was up, but we were just holding on because we had been together for so long. But what sense does that make? Staying in a relationship unhappy? We were kids when we first started out. So now that we were older, we had just grown apart. We were getting along so great as friends that at times when we both would leave the house with bags packed and we would tell each other to drive safe as we would head towards whomever we were dealing with. Things were going great, but we still knew we couldn't continue living together, even if we were friends. So that February, Darius moved out of the apartment.

I had to decide if I was staying in the apartment or moving back into my mom's house. At 22 years old, I didn't want to go back. It was my pride. Going back under someone else's roof wasn't in *my* plans and, honestly, I didn't want to feel like I had failed at something again. What would people say? They would have something to talk about. Yet how was I going to make it work with just me making $12.75 paying $775 a month for rent with a $250 car payment, electricity bill, groceries, toiletries, etc? So, I asked my cousin to move in with me because I knew that would be so much fun! My first cousin Aubrey was like a sister to me. Because we both were our parents' only children, we were extremely close. Things were good in the beginning but that only lasted for a few months and then we started bumping heads. So, she eventually moved out. I don't think either of us were ready. She was a few years younger than me, so there were things she didn't understand, and I was stuck in my own way.

As time went on, I struggled. There were times I had no food in the house. Times I needed gas and didn't know how I would make it home from work. Then there were times when my lights were shut off and I would make up a story about how they were doing work in my apartment so my mom and grandma wouldn't ask any questions when I needed to spend the night.

I knew there was no way I could manage keeping that apartment by myself. I knew from the beginning I should have gone back to my mom's house, but you know how pride gets in the way. I didn't want to give anyone the satisfaction and I didn't want to hear, "I told you so." I was 20 years old when I moved out and people had already doubted me, so to have to move back made me feel like they had won. I was so disappointed in myself. Disappointed that I had become so reliable on D. Disappointed that I had failed my test. Disappointed that I had to go back. But I had to put my pride aside and do what was best for me at that moment. So, I moved back home.

Home Sweet Home

It was May and I packed up my things and placed them in storage and went back to my mom's house. At the time my mom lived two minutes from my job, so it was convenient as I worked and caught up on my bills. I paid off my Infiniti, but it wasn't any good, so I traded it in and got a new car. I was focused on getting back on track. Honestly, I had put the NCLEX to the side because I was afraid of failing again. I had tried numerous times to study but I never went back to retest; For months I was depressed. The thought of me no longer having my home caused me to slip into depression. To go from complete freedom to living under someone else's roof was difficult. Not that my mom was strict because she wasn't, I had freedom, but it still wasn't my own home.

Not too long after my breakup, I started dating this guy. Things started off great as we both were fresh out of previous relationships, but as time went on things started to deteriorate. We had so many similarities and I felt like we could possibly have a bright future together but, I felt like he wanted too much of me. And to be honest, I don't know if we really were connecting like we thought or was it just because we were just coming out of situations, and we used each other to heal. Either way, I knew I was in no position to be settling down with anyone anytime soon. Mentally, I wasn't ready to be settled down with anyone, not just yet. I needed to be by myself and to get myself together. But it still felt like I was missing something, and it wasn't a man.

Something just felt off. I felt like my whole life was crumbling into pieces. I was still struggling. *There is no way I should still be struggling if I'm back home with less bills. How can this be? What is it, Lord, that I need to do?* I knew I needed to get back to getting on track. So, I decided that it was time to get my head back in the game. Desiree had given me some study materials, so I put myself on a study schedule. I woke up at 9:30 am and I would study until noon and then head to work and do it all over again. Day after day, I was in my books.

I called things off with the guy and explained to him that I needed time to focus on me. He didn't quite understand that, but I had to do what was best for me. I felt like God was pulling me away for a reason. It was as if God was trying to get my attention because I felt stuck. I had packed up my apartment and been back home for months and still hadn't made much progress. And that's when it all made sense. God had made me uncomfortable because it was time to make a move. You see, when God is trying to take you to a place and you won't obey Him, He will make you move. He made me so uncomfortable that I had no choice but to obey him.

SECOND TIME'S THE CHARM

In November of 2016, I finally sat for my boards. *Biting my fingernails. Sitting on the edge of my chair. Watching the clock. Question by question.* I got to question 80 and decided to take a break. My stomach was turning as I walked to the bathroom. Sweat dripped off the palms of my hands, I paced back and forth, and I prayed. I prayed for knowledge and understanding of each question. As I walked back to the testing room, I walked with confidence. I got to question 205, the maximum number of questions, and the computer shut off. Three hours and twenty-five minutes is how long it took me. Although I felt confident, more confident than last time, I was still a nervous wreck. I'm a firm believer in moving in silence so not many people knew that I was going to retest. I went home and told my mom that I had taken the NCLEX. Nervously, we kept checking the board of nursing website for what seemed like every thirty minutes.

That next morning, I woke up and typed my name in the Georgia Board of Nurses license look up and there it was–Harper Johnson, Licensed Practical Nurse along with my license number just how I had imagined it. I couldn't believe it. I felt like my time had finally come. I sat there in awe taking in the moment. My mom called everyone in her contacts to tell them, "My baby did it!" At that moment, I knew it was all in His plan. I had fallen dependent on my ex. I wasn't thinking about retesting. We went our separate ways. I struggled and struggled until I realized I had to do something. I obeyed Him, I trusted Him and allowed Him to lead me, and I could now say that I ,Harper J., was a Licensed Practical Nurse. I guess good things do come to those that wait. I had fallen into depression because I thought God had forgotten all about me. I mean it seemed like for a second everyone around me was getting blessed but me.

I remember one scripture my great-grandma used to say all day everyday, Jeremiah 29:11. "For I know the plans I have for you; declares the Lord, plans to prosper you and not to harm you, plans to give you a hope and a future." She said it meant that God already has our life planned out. He already knows our future. But here's the thing. It's on *His* timing. Not ours. God will not give us our blessings until He sees fit. So, while I was thinking He was ignoring me, He was really looking out for me and preparing me. We get so upset when things don't happen when we want it to happen but the whole time God is really looking out for us. I've learned that it doesn't matter how long it takes to get there, as long as you get there. I used to say all the time "I can't do this" or "I can't do that," and grandma Cattie used to say, "Little girl, you watch your mouth. Don't you know there is power in the tongue." I'd just look at her like she was crazy. She would then proceed to say, "Kittie, don't say what you don't mean. Now have some faith. Manifest baby. Speak it into existence."

Those words she said when I was little stuck with me like glue. Whenever I give advice to my girls, I use Grandma Cattie's lines. Before I took my test the second time, I started manifesting. I put it in the atmosphere that I was going to pass. I set passwords as my name with LPN behind it. Sounds crazy, but I did it. Before I went into the testing room, I told myself I was walking in as a certified nurse aide and that I was walking out as a Licensed Practical Nurse. I literally spoke it into existence. This is what you must do. Claim it as if it's already yours. If you speak negatively, negative things will happen. If you speak positively, positive things will happen.

GIRLS NIGHT OUT

Life was good. I was working as a nurse, making great money, paying off bills, you know enjoying the moment that I once prayed for. It was a Saturday night in July and I was going out for some drinks and good music with my homegirls from work, Towanna and Kendra. We were also celebrating Towanna who was a new college graduate. We ended up at a sports bar called *Boogies* and it was jumping. Drinks were on point and we were dancing, playing pool, you know just having a good time as usual. There was a tall, heavy-set, dark-skinned man that happened to be one of the club bouncers. I noticed that he kept looking in my direction. He watched my every move. I didn't know whether to be concerned or flattered. *I'm Still in Love* by Sean Paul came on and I was, well you know, "in my zone." He walked up to me and spoke

"What's your name, Sweetie?"

"I'm Harper, and you?"

After staring me up and down he said, "I'm Ant...Anthony."

The conversation took off from there. We danced and flirted just a little. After all, he was on the job. We talked for a bit, and he shared that he was married but separated. He gave me the whole back story. He told me how they were no longer seeing eye to eye and how they had previously discussed getting a divorce. So, it was pretty clear that's what he was going to do. Did I mention he was 19 years older than me?

I gave him a little bit of my background and the night went on. As the night came to an end, we exchanged numbers and then he leaned forward and poked out his lips. Now usually I would have smacked the taste out of someone, furthermore a stranger that even tried to put their lips on mine, but I shrugged my shoulders and gave him a little peck. I knew I had had one too many for me to do that. The next morning, I received a text from Ant aka "Mr. Wrong," and it read, *"Good morning beautiful."* I smiled as it had been a while since I had had any good morning text messages. We continued to text throughout the day and, honestly, it felt nice to have some attention. I was at a point in life where I was in between the "I'm single and enjoying it, but I also miss having that special person" stage. I kept telling myself that this situation was not going anywhere. I mean even though he was separated and getting a divorce, he was still married, and I was not getting involved with that. And let's not forget the age difference! But it was something about him that kept me interested. A few days went by, and we had planned to see each other one Saturday night after he was off. That night we went to this beautiful area by the water. We walked and talked for hours. I mean he made me laugh just from the simplest conversation. He was so charming. I was enjoying him. Those good times went on and on. Before I knew it a week turned into a month, a month turned into many months, and months turned into a year.

HE LOVES ME.
HE LOVES ME NOT.

It had been a year since I met Mr. Wrong and there were so many good times yet so many broken promises. There were many red flags that I acknowledged but wasn't ready to accept another failed relationship. The time we spent together was great. He was something that I had never experienced before. His maturity, his advice, even his hugs were different. I loved that he was a family man and how he adored his children. His children were from a previous relationship. I felt so protected with him. Yet I never felt the security of the relationship and that was a red flag. It had been over a year that we had been "together" and still something felt off. Plans were not being followed through and something was always "coming up." I had talked with his kids and even been around some family members, but it still did not feel right. I started noticing there were certain times when we could talk and be together. He would make up some story. I would just try to accept it and take his word, even when I knew deep down inside it was a red flag. I just was not ready to accept the truth. I know it sounds familiar right? I had been there for him so many times but when I needed him, he wasn't always there. He would go missing and I wouldn't hear from him until hours later. He blamed a broken phone or a midday nap on his missing whereabouts.

When I started searching for a place, he fed me all these ideas of us becoming a family and moving in together. At his direction, we met with landlords to look at places, but his actions didn't match the words that came out of his mouth. One time we were supposed to move into a condo on March 16th, but something had gone wrong in the apartment. There was an electrical problem so we had to wait for the city to do an inspection and they decided that it would take a month before the issue could be resolved. I had given him half of the first month's rent. When we didn't move in, we decided to keep looking. Time went on and still nothing changed. Still no home. Still searching. Still didn't feel secure in the relationship. Still ignoring red flags.

He sent me a picture of a house and had the audacity to tell me that he had spoken to the landlord, and he offered us a great deal. I noticed from the picture that there was no for rent sign or anything. Towanna and I pulled up to the house and there were people sitting in the living room having a family gathering. It didn't appear that anyone was moving anytime soon. Towanna was the friend that didn't play. She didn't tolerate anything. She was a "straight to the point" kind of person, so when she jumped out the car to go knock on the door, it was no surprise. A lady opened the door and asked, "May I help you?" Towanna asked her if the house was for rent. To our surprise (or maybe not so much), the lady laughed and said, "No ma'am, it isn't." *This doesn't make any sense. Why would he lie?* But I still stayed. Still ignoring red flags.

By then he was supposedly staying with his sister, whom I had never met. I also never knew where she stayed. I only saw pictures of certain parts of the house when he would send me pictures of him and I would examine the background. He fed me a story on how he and his siblings didn't get along that well and that his sister was never happy for him so he didn't want her in his business. His excuses were becoming even more ridiculous on why I could only see him at certain times and it was something he always needed. I was sick of him and sick of giving him my hard earned money. Since I felt like I couldn't really do much financially in my last relationship, I felt like I was obligated to help Mr. Wrong. I had probably given him close to $10k and the money that was used for the first month's rent I never received back. Still, I stayed. This continued, and I had become so mentally drained. I never knew someone could have the power to take over my mind. The relationship sucked me dry. I didn't recognize the person I had become. I didn't know what made me happy anymore. I couldn't eat nor sleep.

My life revolved around him. I had given that man the power to control my emotions, and he knew it. He knew just what to say. I realized that this was not a healthy situation.

I decided that I was going to do things on my own. He had made me lose out on so much. I was approved for a brand new three-bedroom home and because of him it was swiped from me. I wasn't willing to lose out on anything else because of him. I couldn't take it anymore. I was approved for an apartment in Peachtree City, 60 minutes from my job and I did everything myself. He was not there; in fact, he had made up a story about how he was sick and that he wouldn't be able to move his things in the apartment nor help me. At this point, I really didn't want him moving in anyway. I was literally moving boxes into *my* apartment by myself until my family was able to help the next day. I didn't even mention to my friends that Ant was MIA during the process of moving, I was too embarrassed. I told him that I'd had enough of him and the situation and I told him he couldn't move into MY apartment. Of course, he was apologetic and asked if he could work his way back to earning my trust. So, I gave him one last shot despite my feelings of being already done.

One weekend, we had planned to spend the evening together, so I had prepared a big dinner. Ribs, fried chicken, mac n cheese, string beans, potato salad, cornbread and I even baked his favorite cake. Strawberry with vanilla icing. I received a text message–not a phone call–and it read, *"Hey baby, I'm at the ER. Turns out I have an internal bleed."* He went on to say that he was being discharged and going to his sister's house. I couldn't believe it! Well yes I could. I had become so fed up that I didn't care. I knew it was a lie. I knew it was over for me.

Kendra and I had decided to go to our coworker's birthday party that was held at the coworker's cousin's house since my plans didn't follow through with Ant. We pulled up to this beautiful house in a beautiful neighborhood. This house stood out. It was the only house that had a yellow door and yellow garage door. I had a lump in my throat because Ant had sent me a picture of him standing in front of his "sister's house" and in the background was a yellow garage that looked very similar to this one. But I didn't say anything to Kendra. We knocked on the front door and the door cracked open. It was a light-skinned lady that looked like she had gotten ready in the dark because her wig was twisted and her lace was lifted. Kendra looked at me and I looked at her as I knew we were thinking the same thing. We must be at the wrong house.

"Sorry, we have the wrong house," Kendra quickly stated.

"Hey y'all, come on in," a voice said from behind the woman. It was our coworker Shante.

"This is my cousin Daphne. Daphne, these are my girls from work, Harper and Kendra." Daphne had this odd look on her face but I figured she was just having fun, maybe too much fun.

We spoke and went in. There were a lot of people. Shante took us to the kitchen where there were jello shooters, shots of tequila and an alcoholic punch and then we made our way to the garage where the music was blasting. As I walked in, I heard the sound of a familiar voice speaking on the mic.

"I want everyone in here to take a shot for my cousin in-law, Shante!"

My heart nearly jumped out of my chest because I couldn't believe it. It was ANT. We made eye contact and he looked as if his life had flashed before his eyes.

"Girl is that..." Kendra could not even finish her question.

"Yes! A lying son of a..."

"Hey y'all, let me introduce you to my cousin's husband Nate. This is their home, isn't it nice? They just moved here not too long ago." *Seemingly* oblivious to what was going on, Shante was excited to make introductions.

"Nate?! Shante, I'm sorry, but we have to go. Kendra, let's go before things get messy."

As we headed towards the door, Daphne stepped in front of me.

"Hi Harper, nice to finally meet you," she said with a smirk. "Thanks for helping us purchase this house. Isn't it beautiful?"

In walked Ant, I mean Nate, hell I didn't know what to call him.

"Harper, I can explain."

Before I knew it, I had smacked the living shit out of him. Kendra dragged his wife from the living room to the kitchen. Shante was looking at all of us as if she didn't have a clue on what was going on, but I didn't care. As far as I knew, she was a part of these scamming heffas. While Kendra was still working on the wife, Ant was trying to figure out if his face was still attached to his body, so I went after Shante. After that Kendra and I bounced.

"Harp! Harp! Wake up girl! I've been calling you and knocking on the door. I had to use the spare key, I thought something was wrong. I told you I was coming over to get a plate after I got off work."

I had fallen asleep. I didn't know whether to laugh or cry. That was a nightmare. I told Kendra about the dream. She laughed and said, "That's just another confirmation to finally be done with him and especially after the stunt he pulled about him being in the hospital."

Kendra was right. I was done with Ant. I couldn't take it anymore. I felt so ashamed that I even got involved with this man. I had lost so much respect for myself. I was tired of everything. I was sick of being in my twenties. What happened to twenties being the best years of people's lives? Older people would say, "I would pay to be 20 again." Well, I wanted to know what life they were living because it seemed like all I had been doing was failing, going through depression and falling for the wrong guy. Twenties SUCKED, at least for my life anyway. After dwelling on my wrong doings for weeks, I remembered the good things that came out of all the situations I had been through and I stopped complaining. It was all a learning experience that made me stronger and wiser.

WHEN LIFE THROWS YOU LEMONS....

When life throws you lemons, you make lemonade. We all have heard that saying. Well honey, I made a whole pitcher. Now that I was back on my own and Mr. Wrong was out of the picture, I was doing great. The fact that I was doing it all on my own, paying $500 more in rent than my previous apartment meant so much more. I vowed to never lose myself again. Was it easy? Not at all, but with God I knew I would be fine. If there was one thing that I had learned from my mom, it was how to make it as a strong, independent woman. I was working and enjoying my life. Hanging out with the girls and coming home to something that was mine was the best feeling ever. I could honestly say I did it, and it meant so much considering my history. I felt like I could do anything. I may have lost out on money and time from Mr. Wrong, but to have a peace of mind was worth more than anything in this world.

I took time to find Harper again. I got in shape. I changed my lifestyle around and decided to focus my attention on God more. And I loved every bit of it. I loved who I was becoming. I learned that peace was so valuable and important and I vowed to never let anything, or anyone take that away from me. Did I get a little lonely at times? Sure, after all I am human. Some of my friends were in long-lasting relationships, some were engaged and even married. At times, I wondered if I would ever get there, but I knew it was all in His timing. I needed to take time to heal and get back to me. I owed myself this peace.

JAYCEON DOUGLASS

I had been single for a year and I was happier than I've ever been. I wasn't really looking to get into anything too soon because I had had my share of failed relationships. I didn't want to put myself through that anymore and besides it seemed like guys my age were only interested in what was between my legs rather than getting to know ME.

Aubrey was having a shindig one weekend and her boyfriend decided that he wanted to have his homeboy come down to meet me. I told him I wasn't really open to meeting anyone. I had erected a gate around my heart, and I was loving not having to worry about the "what ifs." However, my cousin's boyfriend insisted that his friend and I would be perfect for each other. He noted that we both were headed in good directions. After much thought, I told him he could invite him along.

It was the night of the party and I tried on about 20 different outfits trying to find *the one*. Something that showed my curves but nothing too flashy. I mean, I had never seen this man before, and he was traveling four hours from Savannah to Columbus, Georgia. I didn't know what to expect. I saw a picture of him, but it's different when you are face to face. I arrived at my cousin's house, and we started the party. My cousin's boyfriend slid out to go meet him so that he could follow him back to the house. About 10 minutes later, my aunt said, "They are here, Kittie."

I was so nervous; I felt butterflies in my stomach. In walked my cousin's boyfriend smiling at me and behind him was this tall, light-skinned, bearded, fit guy in a fitted hat, black graphic tee, gray jeans and Jordans. I sized him up from head to toe. He was such a beautiful sight to see. I took a deep swallow and looked up and said, "Thank you, Jesus." Aubrey's boyfriend took him around the room and introduced him to everyone. When they got to me, he hugged me.

"Hello gorgeous. Nice to finally meet you, I'm Jayceon." *Oh my God!* He smelled so good. I didn't want to let him go.

"Hi I'm...I'm..."

"You're Harper," Aubrey said as she slowly shook her head. As she finished my sentence, because clearly, I was stuck in a daze from looking at this beautiful site that was standing in front of me. I thought I was speaking but no words came out. As the night went on, we talked, laughed and joked; it was like we had known each other for years. Everyone got along just fine. He and my mom were even getting along. It was such a blast.

We ended up spending the whole weekend together. That Saturday we went to catch a movie and then grabbed dinner and that Sunday we went to the Coca-Cola Space Science Center. I've always had an interest in museums, so I thought that was a plus that he suggested. We spent time getting to know one another and finally I asked why he wasn't in a relationship. He went on to say that it was because he was a busy individual. He worked and played semi-pro football and had practices, so his time was limited. I respected that because I wasn't looking for anything serious and I was thinking about taking my nursing career in a different direction, so I had my eye on a couple of schools. As the weekend came to an end, we planned to see each other on Tuesday before he headed back to Savannah. I spent time reflecting over that weekend and I remember smiling from ear to ear as I replayed all the events that had taken place. We connected so well. So, I was looking forward to seeing him before he left.

On Tuesday, I waited for him to reach out to me. I waited the entire day. I didn't want to reach out to him first. I didn't want to feel like I was giving in or allowing myself to feel the urge to talk to this person that I had just met. But as the night grew closer, he finally texted me. I was so excited. He kept his word. That meant so much to me because I had no time for inconsistency even though I wasn't quite looking for anything serious I still had no time for games.

TIME WILL TELL

Jayceon had gone back to Savannah. And honestly, I was unsure on what to expect. I was at that place where my life was going well, and I just didn't want to experience anymore toxicity in my life. So, I didn't know if we would, you know, be a thing or not. In the beginning, we did not talk everyday. After all, he was a busy man, so I understood. I was also a hard worker, so I didn't really have time either. But the more we talked, the more I started to develop a strong liking for him and there was not a day that went by that we didn't call, facetime or text each other.

Months had gone past, and we still were connecting strongly. I think we both were unsure about how far we would go because we were four hours apart. I had experienced a long-distance situation before, but it was only an hour and I had since grown into a mature young lady, so I had different feelings. I decided to just let it flow.

Time went on and we were going back and forth visiting each other. Jayceon was patient with me. He wanted to take the time to get to know me and learn who I was before jumping into anything serious. At first, I was offended because I was so used to moving fast and jumping into situations until I realized how problematic that was for me in the past. I was missing the whole picture. This man wanted to get to know me as a person. That let me know that he didn't want his time wasted either. I knew that if we decided to go further, then it was something that we both really wanted to do.

We continued to see each other. I would go to Savannah, and he would come to Peachtree. We would travel together to his away games. I enjoyed watching him play football. He was so good at it so it was no doubt in my mind that he wouldn't make it to the NFL one day. That was his dream. Things kept progressing between us and eventually, we decided to take that step to commit to a relationship.

DECISIONS, DECISIONS

Jayceon and I's relationship was blossoming so smoothly. It had been a while since I felt something so real. He taught me how it felt to be loved properly. Our relationship taught me, and still is teaching me, what a healthy relationship is. I can love him without losing who I am as a person. I can love him without it causing an effect on my daily life. And he supported me in my dreams just as I supported him in his. That meant a lot to me. As our relationship progressed, we continued to travel between our homes, but we knew we would have to make a move because it was becoming hard to be apart from one another.. Growing up, I always put what I wanted last, but since I had grown into this person, I decided to put myself first. It was time that I began worrying less about others and living my life for me. So, I packed up my apartment and moved to Savannah.

The decision to relocate four hours away was not easy. But it was something that I truly wanted to do not only for the sake of our relationship but most importantly for me. Leaving my family, whom I was extremely close to, was one of the hardest things. However, I knew this change would be something good. I had prayed on it. I needed to do this for myself.

First Response

So many great things were happening. It was July of 2019, and Jayceon and I were set to move. We had our move-in date in August, and we were preparing to be in one household. There was so much newness in the air. He was preparing to start his new job, I was preparing to start my new job as a travel nurse, and I was also preparing to return to school in the fall.

One day, I was in Savannah for the week with Jayceon preparing for our move and handling business for my new job. I noticed that I was bleeding and cramping as if it was time for my menstrual. Knowing that mother nature had paid me a visit a week and a half earlier, I knew something was wrong. The cramps became intense, and I was unsure of what was going on. My friend suggested that I take a pregnancy test because of my symptoms. I laughed. I literally cracked up because there was no way I was pregnant. I mean, come on. I had never been pregnant before and besides I was diagnosed with Polycystic Ovarian Syndrome, so I knew that I was not pregnant because I hadn't had any medications or special procedures. Just to make her feel better and prove my point, I decided to test.

To my surprise, two big red lines popped up. PREGNANT! I was so shocked. I could not believe it. Of course, I knew I was doing what it takes to get pregnant, but hear me out! I had never gotten pregnant before. Ever. And to be honest after being with my ex for seven years and never falling pregnant, I thought I was infertile or at least thought I would have to have a procedure or meds to conceive. So many emotions were running through my head.

What should I do? I'm pregnant. Wait, you mean to tell me I didn't have to have help? So, I can conceive naturally? Woah, I'm scared. We are about to move. I'm about to start a new job and so is he. School starts in the fall; how are we going to do this? Jay has football. But I know we have family support. Wait, Harp, you are pregnant, but you are bleeding and cramping. This is not good. Something is wrong. I quickly snapped back into reality.

After I called my mom, I went back into the house to tell Jayceon the news. Both shocked, we sat in silence for a moment and finally he hugged and kissed me and asked if I was okay. Such a sign of relief because I was freaking out. I knew I needed to get to the emergency room ASAP. I Went to the nearest hospital where I was informed that I was in fact in the process of miscarrying. Although we weren't quite ready to be parents, no one wants to be told that they are losing a child. I was crushed. I felt overwhelmed. I wondered why God would let that happen. I was pregnant but it was being swiped from me. Then the questions started flooding my mind. *Will I ever be strong enough to hold a child? What if I have trouble conceiving again?* But I was missing the brighter picture. Here I was thinking I would have trouble conceiving, but God was showing me I could do it when the time is right. He showed me that all things are possible with Him.

New Chapter

After healing from the miscarriage, I relocated to Savannah the next month where Jayceon and I shared our apartment. I stepped out of faith and it was the best decision I've ever made. Things were great. I admit it felt good. I finally felt like my life was coming all together. I was digging this "Twenty thing". School had started and I was enjoying traveling nursing. Prior to moving I had been at my job for eight years because I was afraid of change. But since moving and starting this new job I realized I had been putting limitations on myself. With traveling nursing I worked in facilities in different towns near Savannah. I had learned and experienced so much in such little time. It made me a better nurse. I knew I had made the right decision. This move had boosted my focus level even more. I had a whole different view on life. I knew what I wanted and what it would take to get there. Jay was also enjoying his new job and had become the supervisor of his department. Work, home, school, football and making memories was our life. And I enjoyed every bit of it. I felt like I was living my purpose. These were the times I prayed for.

The Question

Time had flown, before I knew it, we were celebrating year two of being together. Jayceon had decided that we were going out to celebrate our two-year anniversary, not to mention, I graduated the weekend prior from Georgia State University with my bachelor's degree in healthcare management and Jayceon had several different NFL teams looking at him and he was being scouted for a possible draft. I was so proud of us. Following our dreams. It was a dream come true. I learned that no dream is too big.

Jayceon had a nice dinner planned out for us. He told me to be ready by 7:00, and he would come and pick me up. I knew that he had something up his sleeve because he had left me $700 to get my hair, nails and feet done and to buy me something new to wear. I was anxious because I knew he had something up his sleeve and so did I. I had something important to tell him. I had been keeping this secret for a few weeks...actually two secrets.

Seven o'clock came and Jayceon arrived at our front door to pick me up. After driving about 20 miles, we pulled up to this fancy restaurant called Le Bernardin. I was so excited because I'd been dying to go. It was beautiful. He had reserved a table on the rooftop. I had stuffed salmon and he had his favorite– steak. As we stuffed the last bit of our dinner in our mouths, he said, "Harp, I have something to talk to you about."

"So do I."

He proceeded to tell me that he had been drafted by the Dallas Cowboys and he wanted to see how I felt about the offer. I nearly fell out of my seat because I was going to tell him that I was being offered an Executive Director position in Houston. My current place of employment was opening another facility, a 160-bed retirement home and being that I had made several positive changes and the fact that I had finished school, my boss suggested that I apply for the job. I had kept this to myself because ,honestly, I didn't think I would get it. Being an African-American, in my twenties and a female. Not to mention a new graduate and didn't have much experience. I did have some management under my belt but nothing I felt like was enough for someone to give me a chance. I felt like I was getting ahead of myself, but my boss insisted that I applied. She said, "Harper never say what you can't do." I smiled as it reminded me of something great-grandma Cattie would say. Two days later I received the job offer and I was blown away.

Jay congratulated me and I congratulated him. We chuckled at the irony of the situation. I just took it as a confirmation from God. The waitress approached us and said we must be ready for dessert because we seemed to be celebrating. We smiled and said, "We are!" All while staring deeply into each other's eyes.

After dessert, we were preparing to leave. As I grabbed my purse, I heard this loud noise, and it suddenly became windy. I took a step back as I noticed a helicopter coming up from the side of the building and then circling. I reached for Jayceon's hand because I was frightened. "Jay, something must be going on."

While still looking at the sky to see where the helicopter had gone, Jayceon released my hand. I turned to see why and there he was, down on his knee with the most beautiful ring I had ever seen. The helicopter made its way back to view and it had a sign dangling from it. *Will You Marry Me?*

I dropped to my knees and gave Jay the biggest kiss as tears rolled down my face.

"Well baby, is that a yes?"

"Of course, it's a yes!"

As he placed the ring on my finger, I cried even more. He hugged me so tightly. And that's when I shared my second secret.

"I'm pregnant," I whispered in his ear.

He grabbed me even tighter. There was a crowd behind us clapping and cheering us on. Jay blurted out, "She said yes, AND I'm going to be a dad!"

As I looked into the crowd, I noticed familiar faces. My family was there, Desiree and Tevin, Victoria and Deandre, Brianna and Xzavier, Binky, Towanna, Kendra and Jayceon's family. They all had known about this for months.

CHAPTER 29

5 Months Later

I was coming up on my twenty-ninth birthday and we had relocated to Texas. Jayceon and I had purchased a 4-bedroom home. Everything was happening so fast, but it was well worth it. The amount of happiness I was feeling was out of this world. I cried every time I thought about how far I had come. I was about 25 weeks pregnant with twin girls. YES TWINS! Jay was starting his football career that he always dreamed of, and I was heading to my first day of work as the Executive Director at *Plymouth Gardens at Houston*. Before going into work, I decided to stop for a mocha frappe at a nearby coffee shop. There was a bit of a crowd, and it was one customer that was acting a donkey you know what. He was a Caucasian male who looked to be around his late 40s and he was cursing out the lady that had messed up his order.

"Are you stupid? I asked for a caramel frappe and a black coffee, and you gave me mocha. You're pathetic and now I'm going to be late because of you!"

The waitress looked humiliated. I felt so embarrassed for her. She corrected his order and he threw the money on the counter as if she was some sort of dog. I was furious. He stormed out of the shop. I apologized for his behavior and gave her a nice tip. She thanked me, practically in tears. After getting my frappe, I headed to my job. I was so excited yet nervous, but I remembered what grandma always told me, "I can do anything." As I turned into the parking lot of Plymouth Gardens a feeling of peace came over me. I knew I was where I belonged. I pulled into the parking spot that had a sign that read "Executive Director" in front of it. I said a prayer and took a deep breath. *You got this, Harp.*

Just as I opened my car door, I heard what sounded like brakes squealing from behind my SUV. I looked in the rearview mirror and low and behold, it was the guy. The rude guy from the coffee shop. I grabbed my purse and my briefcase and stepped out of my car. I was ready for whatever he was going to throw my way. He stormed out of his vehicle like a mad man. Before I could say anything, he opened his mouth

"Well, well, well. It's you from the coffee shop. And just what do you think you are doing? This parking spot is for the executive director and it sure as hell isn't..." I interrupted him as I extended my hand for a shake.

"Hello, I'm Harper Johnson, the new Executive Director of Plymouth Gardens. And you were saying?"

If you could have seen the look on his face! He had turned pale. He looked as if I were a ghost.

He finally opened his mouth and said, "My apologies, Ms. Johnson I didn't know you were the new ED. I stopped and got you coffee, I always grab coffee for the ED."

"Thank you, but I don't drink black coffee. I prefer a mocha frappe, now if you don't mind, I have a meeting to get to. Oh and sir–" I glanced at my new, rose gold Movado that Jay gifted me to celebrate my first day.

"It looks like you're late."

As I walked into my facility, I smiled because it turns out that life in my twenties isn't so bad after all."

MEET THE AUTHOR

I'm so excited to present to you my very first book! My name is Tieanna Denae Harris. I was born and raised in Franklin, Virginia, but I currently reside in Greensboro, North Carolina. I am twenty six years old and I'm expecting my first child. I am a nurse and now I can also say that I am a writer! How exciting! When I first had the idea of writing a book, I didn't know where to start or which way to go. I thought that this idea would be just that..an idea but I was blessed with the opportunity to work with an amazing publisher, Kristen R. Harris who helped bring my idea to life. Also, the amazing support of my family and friends helped make this all possible. I pray that this book will be an inspiration to all and that this book is the first of many to come.